Will Eva Miss the Party?

"Is your dad going to be OK?" I asked.

Eva nodded. "He's going to be fine. But the worst part is that Dad had to close the restaurant."

Mr. Simpson owns a restaurant right on the beach. It's very popular. Mr. Simpson makes yummy Jamaican food.

"Well, don't worry," I said. "Your dad will be back at work soon."

"I know," Eva said. "But until he is, I don't want to ask my parents for money to buy Lila a birthday present. So I can't go to Lila's party."

Bantam Books in the SWEET VALLEY KIDS series

#1	SURPRISE! SURPRISE!	#30	JESSICA'S UNBURIED TREASURE
#2	RUNAWAY HAMSTER	#31	ELIZABETH AND JESSICA RUN
#3	THE TWINS' MYSTERY TEACHER		AWAY
#4	ELIZABETH'S VALENTINE	#32	LEFT BACK!
#5	JESSICA'S CAT TRICK	#33	CAROLINE'S HALLOWEEN SPELL
#6	LILA'S SECRET	#34	THE BEST THANKSGIVING EVER
#7	JESSICA'S BIG MISTAKE	#35	ELIZABETH'S BROKEN ARM
#8	JESSICA'S ZOO ADVENTURE	#36	ELIZABETH'S VIDEO FEVER
#9	ELIZABETH'S SUPER-SELLING	#37	THE BIG RACE
	LEMONADE	#38	GOOD-BYE, EVA?
#10	THE TWINS AND THE WILD WEST	#39	ELLEN IS HOME ALONE
#11	CRYBABY LOIS	#40	ROBIN IN THE MIDDLE
#12	SWEET VALLEY TRICK OR TREAT	#41	THE MISSING TEA SET
#13	STARRING WINSTON EGBERT	#42	JESSICA'S MONSTER NIGHTMARE
#14	JESSICA THE BABY-SITTER	#43	JESSICA GETS SPOOKED
#15	FEARLESS ELIZABETH	#44	THE TWINS' BIG POW-WOW
#16	JESSICA THE TV STAR	#45	ELIZABETH'S PIANO LESSONS
#17	CAROLINE'S MYSTERY DOLLS	#46	GET THE TEACHER!
#18	BOSSY STEVEN	#47	ELIZABETH THE TATTLETALE
#19	JESSICA AND THE JUMBO FISH	#48	LILA'S APRIL FOOL
#20	THE TWINS GO TO THE HOSPITAL	#49	JESSICA'S MERMAID
#21	JESSICA AND THE SPELLING-BEE	#50	STEVEN'S TWIN
	SURPRISE	#51	LOIS AND THE SLEEPOVER
#22	SWEET VALLEY SLUMBER PARTY	#52	JULIE THE KARATE KID
#23	LILA'S HAUNTED HOUSE PARTY	#53	THE MAGIC PUPPETS
#24	COUSIN KELLY'S FAMILY SECRET	#54	STAR OF THE PARADE
#25	LEFT-OUT ELIZABETH	#55	THE JESSICA AND ELIZABETH
#26	JESSICA'S SNOBBY CLUB		SHOW
#27	THE SWEET VALLEY CLEANUP	#56	JESSICA PLAYS CUPID
	TEAM	#57	NO GIRLS ALLOWED
#28	ELIZABETH MEETS HER HERO	#58	LILA'S BIRTHDAY BASH
#29	ANDY AND THE ALIEN		

SWEET VALLEY KIDS SUPER SNOOPER EDITIONS
#1   THE CASE OF THE SECRET SANTA
#2   THE CASE OF THE MAGIC CHRISTMAS BELL
#3   THE CASE OF THE HAUNTED CAMP
#4   THE CASE OF THE CHRISTMAS THIEF
#5   THE CASE OF THE HIDDEN TREASURE
#6   THE CASE OF THE MILLION-DOLLAR DIAMONDS
#7   THE CASE OF THE ALIEN PRINCESS

SWEET VALLEY KIDS SUPER SPECIAL EDITIONS
#1   TRAPPED IN TOYLAND
#2   THE EASTER BUNNY BATTLE

SWEET VALLEY KIDS

LILA'S BIRTHDAY BASH

Written by
Molly Mia Stewart

Created by
FRANCINE PASCAL

Illustrated by
Ying-Hwa Hu

BANTAM BOOKS
NEW YORK • TORONTO • LONDON • SYDNEY • AUCKLAND

RL 2, 005-008

LILA'S BIRTHDAY BASH
A Bantam Book / May 1995

*Sweet Valley High® and Sweet Valley Kids are
trademarks of Francine Pascal*

Conceived by Francine Pascal

*Produced by Daniel Weiss Associates, Inc.
33 West 17th Street
New York, NY 10011*

Cover art by Susan Tang

ISBN: 0-553-48209-2

Published simultaneously in the United States and Canada

*Bantam Books are published by Bantam Books, a division of Bantam
Doubleday Dell Publishing Group, Inc. Its trademark, consisting of the
words "Bantam Books" and the portrayal of a rooster, is Registered in the
U.S. Patent and Trademark Office and in other countries. Marca
Registrada. Bantam Books, 1540 Broadway, New York, New York 10036.*

PRINTED IN THE UNITED STATES OF AMERICA

CWO   0 9 8 7 6 5 4 3 2 1

To Jeanne and Burt Rubin

CHAPTER 1

The Best Party Ever

Hi! I'm Elizabeth Wakefield. I am seven years old.

My sister Jessica is also seven years old. We're identical twins. That means we have the exact same birthday. It also means we look exactly alike.

Jessica has blue-green eyes. So do I. And we both have long blond hair with bangs. We always wear name bracelets so that people can tell us apart. Of course, Mom and Dad and Steven always know who is Elizabeth and who is Jessica. Well, *almost* always.

Steven is our big brother. He's two

years older than me and Jessica. He's always teasing us. He calls us shrimps.

Jessica and I are in the same class at school. We even sit next to each other! We go to Sweet Valley Elementary School, and our teacher is Mrs. Otis. She's the best teacher in the world.

I love school. My favorite subject is reading. I can't wait to be older so I can be a writer. I'm already practicing—I write stories all the time. My favorite writer is Angela Daley. Jessica doesn't have a favorite writer. Her favorite part of school is recess. She likes to play "teenagers" with her friends.

Some of my friends at school are Amy Sutton and Todd Wilkins. Lila Fowler and Ellen Riteman are two of Jessica's friends. Jessica and I both like to play with Eva Simpson.

I think Jessica's friends are silly. She thinks I'm crazy to be friends with a boy. Eva is the only one who always gets along with both of us.

Lots of our friends are surprised that Jessica and I are so different. They think identical twins should have identical thoughts. But that's silly. I wouldn't like it if there were two of me!

Even though we like different things, Jessica and I will always be best friends. We love being twins. And we especially love having the same birthday. It's double special!

When Jessica and I turned seven, we invited all of our friends to a party. We played games and ate cake. It was fun, but it was nothing like the party Lila had on her birthday. Lila's party was much bigger and fancier. It also caused a lot more trouble.

"Guess what?" Lila said.

"What?" Amy asked.

We were on the playground after lunch. Eva, Jessica, Lila, and I were playing on the swings. Amy was waiting for a turn.

"I'm going to have pony rides at my birthday party," Lila said. "Daddy made the plans yesterday."

"Real ponies?" Eva asked.

Eva is from Jamaica. That's an island in the Caribbean. Mrs. Otis showed it to us on a map when Eva moved to Sweet Valley. She had only lived here for a few months. But she already had lots of friends.

"Of course!" Lila exclaimed.

"Wow," Amy said. "That will be fun."

"I know," Lila said in her know-it-all voice.

"Why are you having ponies?" Jessica asked. "You don't like horses."

"But I do like presents," Lila said. "Especially big ones. And if I have a fancy party, everyone will have to get me really big presents!" Lila dragged her feet so that her swing stopped.

"Are you done swinging?" Amy asked eagerly.

"Yes," Lila said. "I want to jump rope now. Come on, Jessica."

Jessica shook her head. "I want to swing some more."

"OK," Lila said. She headed across the playground by herself.

Amy sat down in the empty swing. "When is Lila's party anyway?" she asked. Lila was inviting everyone in Mrs. Otis's class to her party. But we hadn't gotten any invitations yet.

"It's in two weeks and two days," Jessica said.

"That's a long time away," I said.

"I can't wait," Amy said.

"I can't wait for the party for *two* reasons," Jessica announced.

"Two reasons?" I asked.

"Right," Jessica said. "One reason is that Lila's party is going to be the best ever."

"What's the other reason?" Amy asked.

"Because I'm tired of hearing Lila brag," Jessica said.

Amy and I laughed.

"Look at Lila now," Amy said. She pointed across the playground.

Lila was standing in the spot where we always jump rope. But she wasn't jumping, she was talking. Ellen and Suzie Nichols were listening to her. They looked excited.

"I bet she's telling them about the ponies," Eva said.

Jessica nodded. "Lila hasn't talked about anything but the party in days. Did she tell you about the clowns?"

Amy and I nodded.

"And the magician?" Jessica asked.

We nodded again.

"Maybe he'll magically make Lila be quiet," Amy suggested.

Jessica and I giggled.

I realized Eva hadn't said anything

7

for a while. I looked over at her. She had stopped swinging. She was kicking up the dirt under her swing.

"Are you excited about the magician, Eva?" I asked. Eva has a magic set that she really loves. We always play with it when we're at her house.

Eva shrugged. "I guess so."

"Maybe the magician can teach you some new tricks," I said.

"Maybe," Eva said. She pushed off and started to swing again.

"Lois told me Lila is going to fill her pool with ice cream," Amy said. Lois Waller is a girl in our class. She really likes ice cream.

"That's not true," Jessica said. "But there will be lots of good things to eat."

"Like pizza?" I asked.

Jessica nodded. "And hot dogs and popcorn and cotton candy."

"Yummy," I said.

"I'm not going to have time to eat,"

Amy said. "I'm going to spend all of my time with the ponies." Amy and I both love horses—and ponies are almost as good.

"Jim Sturbridge can't come to the party," Jessica said.

"Why not?" Amy asked.

"His family is going to San Francisco," Jessica told us. "They're going to be away all weekend."

"Poor Jim," I said. "I'd hate to miss the party."

"Me, too," Jessica agreed.

Amy nodded.

Eva didn't say anything. I turned to look at her.

"Wow," I exclaimed. "You're really going high, Eva!"

While the rest of us watched, Eva pushed her swing even higher. Then she jumped off. When she hit the ground, she fell forward on her hands and knees.

"Are you OK?" I called.

Eva didn't answer. She just got up and walked away without saying a word.

Jessica and Amy and I traded looks.

"What's wrong with Eva?" Amy whispered.

"I'll find out," I said. I jumped off my swing and ran after her.

CHAPTER 2

A Serious Problem

"Eva!" I called.

She was walking across the playground really fast.

"Hey, Eva!" I yelled. "Wait for me."

Eva stopped walking. But she didn't turn to face me. Her eyes were on the ground.

I ran to catch up. "Is something wrong?"

Eva turned toward me. Her eyes were filled with tears. "I'm fine," she said.

"No, you're not," I said. "Listen, you don't have to tell me what's the matter. But it might make you feel better."

"You have to promise not to tell," Eva said.

"I promise," I said.

"Not even Jessica," Eva insisted.

"Cross my heart," I assured her.

Eva looked around. "Come cn."

She led me to the other side of the playground where it's dark and gloomy. Not many kids play there.

"What's the matter?" I asked.

Eva took a shaky breath. "My dad hurt his back."

"Oh, no," I said. Poor Eva. I would feel terrible if my dad got hurt. "Is your dad going to be OK?" I asked.

Eva nodded. "He's going to be fine. But the doctor says he has to stay in bed until his back is all better."

"Yuck," I said. "I hate staying in bed when I'm sick."

"Me too," Eva said. "But that's not the worst part. The worst part is that Dad had to close the restaurant."

Mr. Simpson owns a restaurant right on the beach. It's very popular. That's because Mr. Simpson is an excellent cook. He makes yummy Jamaican food.

"Can't your mom run the restaurant?" I asked.

Eva shook her head. "She has to work." Mrs. Simpson plays the flute in the orchestra.

"Maybe we can help," I suggested.

Eva shook her head. "There are plenty of people to wait tables and stuff like that. But there's nobody to cook."

"Oh," I said. "I don't think we could do that."

"No," Eva replied. "Nobody but Dad can."

"Well, don't worry," I said. "Your dad will be back at work soon."

"I know," Eva said. "But until he is, I don't want to ask my parents for money to buy Lila a present. And Dad's going to be in bed for at least two

weeks. So I can't go to Lila's party."

I gasped. "Don't your parents have money?"

"Yeah, they do," Eva said. "We have enough for food and bills and important stuff—I heard my mom say so. But Lila wants expensive presents. I can't get her anything like that."

"But the party is going to be so much fun," I told her. "You can't miss it."

"I don't want to," Eva said. "But I can't go without a present."

"Maybe you should tell Lila about your dad," I suggested.

"No way," Eva said. "Lila would never understand."

Eva was probably right about that. Lila is rich and spoiled rotten. She always gets whatever she wants—no matter what it costs.

"Remember," Eva said. "You promised not to tell."

"I know," I answered.

"Not even Jessica," Eva reminded me.

"OK," I said.

"And not Mrs. Otis," Eva added. "Or any other adults."

"But maybe Mrs. Otis could help," I argued.

"No!" Eva said. "She might call my parents. I don't want them to worry about me. And the other kids might make fun of me."

"I promise not to tell," I said. "But maybe I can help you think of a way you can buy a present and come to the party."

Eva nodded. "I'll think about it, too."

CHAPTER 3

Too Many Dolls

The next morning before class started, I was reading a book at my desk. Jessica was in the front of the room. She was talking to Lila—about her party, no doubt. Jessica looked bored.

"Hi, Elizabeth," Eva said.

"Hello!" I said. "You look happy."

"I am!" Eva lowered her voice. "I can come to the party. I thought of something to give Lila."

"You did?" I asked.

Eva nodded. "I thought of it last night in bed. See, I have this fancy doll I call Stella. She sits on a shelf across the room from my bed. Mom and Dad gave her to me last Christmas."

"I think I've seen her," I said. "She has black hair, right?"

"Right!" Eva said.

"She's really beautiful," I said.

Eva smiled. "She sure is! *And* I've never played with her. She's just like new. Which is perfect! Because now I can give her to Lila for her birthday."

"Are you sure?" I asked. "Stella sounds really special."

"Stella *is* special," Eva said. "But not as special as Lila's party. I really, really want to go. I've got to see that magician."

I grinned. "Well, if you're sure—I'm glad you're coming!"

"Me, too," Eva said.

Mrs. Otis arrived, and school started. Eva did all her work with a big smile on her face. I even heard her humming!

When the bell rang for morning recess, Eva and I ran outside together.

"What should we play?" I asked.

"Let's go on the jungle gym," Eva said. "I want to climb to the very top!"

Eva and I ran to the jungle gym. We got there before anyone else. We climbed the ladder to the very top. Then we sat down. We could see the entire playground.

"Here comes Amy," I said.

"And Ellen," Eva said.

"And Jessica," I added.

Amy got to the jungle gym before the others. She climbed up to the monkey bars. Then she started to swing across them.

Ellen pulled herself onto the high trapeze.

Jessica got onto the low one.

"Where's Lila?" Ellen called up to me and Eva.

I looked around the playground, but I didn't spot her.

"I see her!" Eva said.

"Where?" I asked.

19

"Over there." Eva pointed. "She's talking to Andy Franklin and Winston Egbert."

"She is?" Ellen sounded surprised.

I was surprised, too. Lila is snobby. She usually says she's too good for Winston and Andy. She thinks they're nerds.

"I know why she's talking to them," Jessica said.

"Why?" Ellen asked.

"Her friends already know all about her party," Jessica said. "She needs some new people to brag to."

"Well, since Lila isn't around, I can tell you a secret," Ellen said. "I got Lila the best present ever!"

"I bet it's not better than mine," Eva said.

"What did you get her?" Ellen asked.

"You tell first," Eva said.

"I got her a Madame Zelda doll," Ellen said.

"What's that?" Amy asked. She hardly ever plays with dolls.

"It's a doll," Ellen explained. "But not a baby doll. It's the kind of doll you're not supposed to touch."

"What good is that?" Amy asked.

"You're supposed to collect them," Ellen said.

"That's stupid," Amy said. "I'd rather have a doll I could play with. That doesn't seem like such a good present to me."

"Well, you're wrong!" Ellen was getting mad. "It's a great present. It was the most expensive doll in the toy department."

"Wow," Jessica said. "That sounds like a really good present to me."

"It is," Ellen said. "The doll was completely handmade. That's why it cost so much."

Suzie Nichols ran up to the jungle gym. "Who wants to jump rope?"

Jessica jumped down. "I do."

"Me, too," Ellen said.

"Not me," Amy said. "I'm going to play dodge ball."

The other girls ran off.

"What do you want to do now?" I asked Eva.

"I don't care," Eva said. Her gloomy face was back.

"What's wrong?" I asked.

"Ellen's doll sounds just like Stella," Eva said. "I can't give Lila the same thing Ellen is."

"Why not?" I asked.

"How would you feel if you got two of the same thing for your birthday?" Eva asked.

"I wouldn't like it," I admitted.

"Now I can't go to the party," Eva said sadly.

I felt sad, too. I knew Eva wanted to see the magician. Besides, almost everyone else in our class was going to the party. *All* of the girls were. I didn't want Eva to feel left out. I had to think of a way to help her.

"Remember when Mrs. Otis got married?" I asked.

Eva nodded.

"Jessica and I earned the money for her present," I said. "Maybe you could earn the money for Lila's present."

Eva smiled. "That's a great idea! What could I do?"

"Jessica and I had a lemonade stand," I said.

Eva's shoulders slumped. "There's a boy on my street who has a lemonade stand every single Saturday."

"Maybe we could steal some of his business," I said.

"Then neither of us would make much money," Eva said.

"You could walk dogs," I suggested.

"Dogs make me sneeze," Eva replied.

"Well, what jobs do you do at home?" I asked.

"Empty the garbage cans," Eva said.

"I don't think anyone will pay us to do that," I said.

"I washed the car once," Eva said. "That was fun. Dad and I had a water fight."

"That's a good idea," I said. "Grown-ups don't like to wash cars. I bet lots of them would pay us to do it."

"You want to help?" Eva asked.

"Sure," I said.

"Great!" Eva exclaimed. "As soon as I get home, I'll ask Mom if we can have a car wash."

CHAPTER 4

Washed-up Car Wash

Eva's parents said it was OK if we had a car wash. They didn't know what Eva was planning to do with the money. That was a secret only Eva and I knew. I didn't even tell Jessica.

Jessica thought I was crazy to work on Saturday. When I left our house early in the morning, she was watching TV in her pajamas.

Mom drove me over to the Simpsons' and dropped me off.

I ran up the walk and rang the doorbell.

"Good morning, Elizabeth," Mrs. Simpson said as she let me in. She had a nice voice, just like Eva's. "Are you ready to wash cars?"

I nodded. "I brought some rags from home. And I even found a can of car wax."

"Good for you," Mrs. Simpson said.

"How's Mr. Simpson?" I asked.

"A little better," Mrs. Simpson said. "Thanks for asking."

Eva came down the stairs. She was carrying a big, colorful sign. It said: CaR WaSH $2.

"That looks great," I told her.

"Thanks," Eva said. "I made it with my Magic Markers."

Eva and I carried her sign outside. Eva leaned the sign against a tree right next to the sidewalk. Everyone driving by would be able to see it.

"I bet we have a lot of customers soon," Eva said.

"We'd better get ready," I said.

"Yeah," Eva agreed. "Let's hurry."

Eva and I pulled the hose out toward the street. We gathered sponges, towels, and soap from inside.

I took out of a bag the rags and wax I had brought.

"We should charge extra for wax," I said. "Rubbing it in is a lot of work."

"OK," Eva agreed.

We sat down on the curb to wait for customers.

"Where is everyone?" Eva asked after a minute.

"They'll be here," I said.

We waited some more.

Eva studied the sky. "Do you think it's going to rain?"

"No!" I said right away. Then I looked up. There *were* a lot of clouds, but they weren't that dark. I crossed my fingers and hoped it didn't rain.

A woman drove up in a shiny white

car. She stopped right in front of us.

"Good morning, girls," the woman said. She climbed out of her car. "Would you like to wash my car while I visit a friend across the street?"

"Sure," Eva said. "But it will cost you two dollars."

"That's fine," the woman said.

"Wax is fifty cents extra," I added.

"Just the wash," the woman decided. "No wax today."

"OK," I agreed.

The woman rolled up her windows so we wouldn't get the inside of her car wet. Then she crossed the street. She rang the doorbell at one of Eva's neighbor's houses.

"Let's get to work," Eva said.

Eva sprayed one side of the car with water.

I soaped it up.

We were rinsing that side when it started to sprinkle.

"Oh, no!" Eva said. "What should we do?"

"Let's just keep going," I suggested. "It's not raining very hard."

But just then the woman who owned the car came out of the house across the street. She started to run toward us.

"It's raining," the woman called. "You might as well quit."

Eva and I traded sad looks.

Since we were half-done, the woman paid us one dollar. Eva put the money in her pocket.

The woman moved her car into the driveway on the other side of the street.

"Maybe the rain will stop soon," Eva said hopefully.

"It will," I agreed.

We sat back down on the curb to wait for our next customer. The ground was damp.

It didn't start to rain any harder. But it also didn't stop. Neither did any cars.

After a while Mrs. Simpson came out onto the porch. "How's it going, girls?" she called.

"Terrible," Eva called back.

"I don't think anyone will want their car washed in the rain," Mrs. Simpson called.

"We want to wait and see," Eva told her.

"OK," Mrs. Simpson said. "Just come in if you get cold."

We waited a few minutes longer. Then Eva got up and walked down to look at her sign. She held it up for me to see. All of the words were blurred. The Magic Marker ink had run in the rain.

I groaned. "Nobody is going to stop now."

"I know," Eva said. "Come on. I give up."

Eva and I gathered all of the car-washing equipment. We went into the house and up to Eva's room.

"I'm sorry about the rain," I said.

Eva shrugged. "It's not your fault."

"Maybe we can think of another plan," I suggested.

"Maybe." Eva didn't sound very hopeful.

I walked over to a shelf. "Is that Stella?"

"Yes," Eva said.

"She's really pretty," I said.

"I can't believe someone made her by hand," Eva said.

"I know," I answered. "That makes her even more special."

Eva nodded.

"Oh, wow," I said. "I just had a great idea."

"What?" Eva asked.

"Why don't you *make* something for Lila?" I asked.

"I don't know how to make anything," Eva said.

"Are you sure?" I asked.

Eva thought for a minute. "Well, my friends and I used to make shell necklaces in Jamaica. But they aren't fancy."

"That doesn't matter," I said. "Shell necklaces are pretty."

"Besides, homemade isn't as good as store-bought," Eva said. "Lila won't like it."

"Come on, Eva," I said. "Don't you want to go to the party? Don't you want to see the magician?"

Eva sighed. "Oh, OK. I'll make a necklace."

"And you'll come to the party," I asked.

"Only if the necklace comes out pretty," Eva said.

I grinned. "We're going to have a great time."

"If I come," Eva said.

CHAPTER 5

Jessica Is Jealous

"You're going to love my gift," Ellen told Lila.

It was lunchtime. Lila, Ellen, Jessica, and I were waiting to buy milk.

"What is it?" Lila asked.

"That's a secret," Ellen said.

"Ellen is driving me crazy," Jessica whispered to me. "She keeps bragging about her stupid present."

"And Lila keeps bragging about her party," I added.

"That's true," Jessica said. "But Ellen is just as bad."

Jessica was right. Lila and Ellen both

bragged all afternoon. By the time we got onto the bus to go home, Jessica looked very grumpy.

Ellen rides our school bus. She sat in front of us.

"I can't wait to get home," Ellen said.

Jessica and I didn't say anything.

"Mom's buying me some special wrapping paper at work," Ellen went on. Mrs. Riteman works at the Sweet Valley Museum. There's a neat gift shop there.

Jessica and I still didn't say anything.

"It's shiny silver!" Ellen told us. "She's also getting a ribbon that's already tied in a bow!"

"That's nice," I said.

Jessica poked me.

"What kind of wrapping paper are you using?" Ellen asked.

"Who knows?" Jessica burst out. "Lila's party isn't for almost two weeks. We haven't even bought a present yet."

"Oh," Ellen said.

We had reached her stop.

Ellen stood up. "Well, you'd better get busy. It will take a long time to find wrapping paper as nice as mine." Ellen skipped down the aisle and jumped off the bus.

Jessica was angry. "I'm going to show that Little Miss Show-off," she said. "I'm going to get something better than a dumb doll for Lila. Something that's twice as expensive."

"It's the thought that counts," I said.

Jessica gave me a funny look. "You sound like Mom. Or Grandma!"

My face heated up. "What I mean is, it doesn't matter how much money you spend."

Jessica laughed. "Of course it does!"

"Well, I don't think Mom and Dad will spend too much," I said.

"Yes, they will," Jessica said.

"How do you know?" I asked.

"Because I'm going to talk them into it," Jessica said.

Jessica talked to our parents that evening at dinner. "Mommy," she started, "what can we buy Lila for her birthday?"

Mom thought for a second. "How about a water toy?"

"That's a neat idea," I said. "Lila could use it in her pool or at the ocean."

Jessica shook her head. "Lila doesn't like water toys."

"How about a book?" Dad suggested.

"No way," Jessica said. "Too boring."

"I don't think books are boring," I said. "They're my favorite presents."

"But it's not *your* birthday," Jessica said. "It's Lila's. And she doesn't want a book."

"Get her a board game," Steven mumbled. His mouth was stuffed with macaroni and cheese.

Jessica wrinkled her nose. "Board games are OK. But we want to get Lila something really special. Right, Elizabeth?"

"Um . . . yeah," I said.

"Like what?" Dad asked.

"Like a diamond ring," Jessica said.

Steven laughed. Then he started to cough. He had just taken a big gulp of milk.

"Are you OK?" Mom asked Steven.

Steven nodded. "What are you going to do, Jessica?" he asked. "*Marry* Lila?"

"Ha, ha," Jessica said.

"A diamond ring is much too expensive," Mom said. "But I'll take you girls shopping over the weekend. I'm sure we'll find something you like."

"Well, Elizabeth and I were talking," Jessica said. "We want to spend the money from our piggy bank."

"There's enough in there for a diamond ring?" Steven asked.

Jessica didn't pay any attention to Steven. She turned to Mom. "If we put our money in with what you were going to spend, we can get something more expensive—I mean, *nicer*."

I gave Jessica an angry look. She was lying. We hadn't talked about spending our piggy-bank money. I didn't want to.

"That sounds fine," Mom said.

"It's your money," Dad said. "You can spend it however you like."

"No, I can't," I mumbled.

"What did you say?" Mom asked.

"May I be excused?" Jessica said quickly. "I want to go count our money."

"Your dad made dessert," Mom said.

Jessica was already on her feet. "I'll eat it later."

"OK," Mom said.

Jessica took off up the stairs.

"May I be excused?" I asked.

"Sure," Mom said.

I ran upstairs. By the time I got to our room, Jessica had already opened the bank. She was sitting on her bed, surrounded by pennies and nickels and dimes. Mostly pennies.

"How could you lie like that?" I asked Jessica.

"I didn't think you'd mind," Jessica said with an innocent face.

"Well, I do," I said. "I don't want to spend my half of the money. I'm saving it to buy a new book."

Jessica's smile faded. "Please? Getting a good gift is really important to me."

"Mom and Dad will buy us a nice present for Lila," I argued.

"But if we put in our money, it will be even nicer," Jessica said. "Come on, Lizzie. Pretty please?"

"Oh, OK!" I said.

"Great!" Jessica said. "Help me count the money."

"It looks like a lot," I said.

"I know," Jessica answered happily.

But when we finished counting, she didn't look as happy.

"I guess it really wasn't that much," I said.

"Two dollars and thirteen cents," Jessica said. "It's not even enough to make a difference."

"Then maybe we should put it back in the bank," I suggested.

Jessica covered the money with her hand. "No! I'm not giving up yet. Somehow I'm going to get Lila a better present than Ellen's. And I might need this money."

CHAPTER 6

On the Beach

"Hi, Elizabeth," Eva said on Saturday morning. She was standing on my doorstep. "Are you ready to go?"

"Yes," I said. "Let me just tell Dad I'm leaving."

"OK," Eva said.

I stuck my head inside the door. "Eva's here!" I yelled. "See you later!"

"'Bye, honey," Dad yelled back. "Have fun!"

Eva skipped down the walk in front of me.

"You're in a good mood," I said.

"I know," Eva said. "That's because my dad is feeling much better."

"Really?" I asked. "Can he go back to the restaurant?"

"Not yet," Eva said. "But maybe soon."

"That's great," I said. "Listen, Eva, we can't go to Sweet Valley Beach today."

"Why not?" Eva asked.

"Jessica is there," I explained. "She went with Lila and her dad this morning."

"We don't want to see them," Eva said.

I shook my head. "That would spoil the surprise."

Eva and I climbed into the Simpsons' car.

"Hi, Elizabeth," Mrs. Simpson said. She was wearing her bathing suit, a blue shirt, and a big floppy hat.

"Hi," I said.

"Can we go to the beach near the restaurant?" Eva asked. That beach is far away from Sweet Valley Beach—two whole miles. "We want to collect shells. There are always good ones there."

"OK," Mrs. Simpson agreed. She drove to the beach, and parked in the restaurant's parking lot. The lights in the building were out.

"The restaurant looks sad," Mrs. Simpson said.

Eva nodded. "It misses Daddy."

"He'll be back soon," I said.

We got out of the car and walked across the sand together.

"This is a good spot," Eva announced.

Mrs. Simpson spread out her towel, lay down, and opened a book.

"Come on," Eva said to me. "Let's look for shells."

Eva and I walked closer to the water. Then Eva led the way down the beach. I picked up shell after shell. Pretty soon I had collected as many as I could carry.

"Hey, Eva!" I called. "I already have enough shells for a necklace."

Eva came closer. She was carrying only four shells. I held out my hands. Eva examined my shells. She started to pick them out one by one and drop them into the sand.

"What are you doing?" I demanded.

"I can't use most of these," Eva said. "The broken ones won't stay on the thread. And some of them are too sharp. I don't want my necklace to hurt Lila."

"Oh," I said.

Eva kept picking through my shells.

"What's wrong with that one?" I asked. "It wasn't sharp or broken."

Eva looked embarrassed. "Nothing's wrong with it. It's just an ugly color."

"What do you mean?" I asked.

Eva held out her hand. "See? All of these are about the same color pink. I think it will look pretty with Lila's hair."

"I see," I said. And I did. The shells Eva had picked really were the best.

Eva chose three shells out of my collection. Then we started to look again. I didn't pick up as many shells as before. It was hard to find ones that were just the right color.

"Are you still looking for shells?" Mrs. Simpson called about an hour later. She had followed us down the beach.

"Yes," I said. My eyes were still on the sand.

Eva showed her mother the shells we had collected. She told her we wanted to make a necklace out of them.

Mrs. Simpson helped us look. She had finished her book. When the three of us had finally collected enough shells, we drove to the Simpsons' house.

Eva and Mrs. Simpson went upstairs to say hello to Mr. Simpson. He was still stuck in bed.

When Eva and her mother came

downstairs, Mrs. Simpson washed the shells. She spread them on the kitchen counter to dry.

We had ham sandwiches and noodle soup for lunch. Mrs. Simpson took a tray to Mr. Simpson. By the time we were finished eating, the shells were dry.

Mrs. Simpson threaded a needle. "This is good strong thread," she said. "Your necklace should last a long time."

Eva carefully strung the shells onto the thread, one at a time.

I watched.

"I'm going to make the necklace long," Eva told me. "That way it will fit over Lila's head."

After she had threaded all the shells, Eva cut the needle off the thread. She tied the ends together.

"Finished!" Eva announced.

"It's beautiful," I told her.

"Not like a Madame Zelda doll," Eva said.

"I think it's better than a doll," I said.

Eva shrugged.

"Are you going to come to the party?" I asked.

"I don't know," Eva said.

"Please come," I pleaded.

"We'll see," Eva said.

CHAPTER 7

Jessica Is a Pain

"How about this?" Mom asked. She took a purple jean jacket off a rack and held it up.

It was Sunday. Jessica, Mom, and I were shopping for Lila's birthday present.

"It's pretty," I said. "Let's get it."

"You didn't even look at it!" Jessica cried.

Jessica was right. I *hadn't* looked at it. We had already been at the mall for hours. I was bored and tired. I wanted to go home.

"Sorry," I said.

"That jacket is ugly," Jessica told Mom.

Mom sighed. "We've already been to the toy store. And all of your favorite clothing stores. You're being awfully picky, Jessica."

"I told you," Jessica said. "I want to get Lila something really special."

"Let's go to the magic shop," I suggested.

"Good idea," Jessica agreed.

Mom, Jessica, and I walked down the mall and into the magic shop. It was crammed full of neat stuff.

"Look at this!" I said. "A magician's cape!"

The cape was black on the outside. It had a red collar that stood up. The lining was covered with stars. It looked like something a real magician would wear. But it was kid-sized.

"It's beautiful," Jessica said.

I nodded.

Mom picked up the tag and read the price. "Sorry, kids. This costs more than two hundred dollars."

"Wow!" I said. "That's a lot of money."

"I don't care how much it costs," Jessica said. "I want it."

"No," Mom said firmly.

After that Jessica wouldn't look at the fortune-telling cards. Or the magic wands. Or anything else in the entire shop. She was pouting.

"Come on, Jessica," I whispered. "You're being a brat."

"Am not!" she said.

"Look at this magic set," I said. "Eva has one just like it. It's really fun. I'm sure Lila would like it."

"I don't want to get Lila something Eva already has," Jessica said. "That's boring."

Mom sighed. "I think we're wasting our time here. Let's go home."

"OK," I said.

53

"No!" Jessica cried. "We can't. We need a present for Lila."

"We'll come back later in the week," Mom promised. "OK?"

Jessica didn't answer.

"OK?" Mom asked again.

"OK," Jessica whispered.

Mom led the way out of the magic store, and down the mall. Jessica and I followed. Jessica was stamping her feet. But then she skidded to a stop.

"Look!" Jessica yelled. She was peering into the window of a store filled with computers and computer supplies.

Mom came back. "What is it?"

"That!" Jessica was grinning. "It is absolutely the most perfect present ever!"

"A disk drive?" Mom sounded confused.

"No, next to that!" Jessica yelled.

"PizzaFace Three," I read off the rectangular box.

"PizzaFace?" Mom asked.

"It's a video game," I explained.

"It's Lila's favorite video game," Jessica said.

"I don't understand," Mom said. "If it's her favorite, then she must already own it."

"No, she doesn't!" Jessica said. "This is PizzaFace *Three*. Lila has PizzaFace *Two*. Three is much better. Ellen said it has a lot more toppings in it. Even anchovies!"

Mom smiled. "Anchovies, huh? Well, we'd better find out how much it is."

The three of us went into the store. Mom talked to a salesman while Jessica and I looked at the game.

After a minute, Mom walked over to us. She was frowning. "I'm sorry, girls. But the game costs more than I want to spend."

"Even with our two dollars and thirteen cents?" Jessica asked.

Mom nodded.

"A lot more?" Jessica asked.

"Enough more," Mom said. "Come on. Let's go."

Jessica didn't move. "Can't we please get it, Mom?" she begged.

"No," Mom said.

"We'll never, ever find a better present," Jessica whined.

"We're not getting it," Mom said.

Jessica crossed her arms. "I bet if it was my birthday, Mr. Fowler would let Lila get PizzaFace Three for me."

"Well, I'm not Mr. Fowler," Mom said. I could tell she was getting angry.

I thought about Eva and her home-made necklace. I didn't think Jessica was being very nice.

"Please?" Jessica pulled on Mom's arm. "I'll do anything."

The salesman turned and stared at us.

"Please," Jessica said quietly.

"Oh, OK," Mom said.

"Yes!" Jessica yelled.

"But I'm not giving you the money,"

Mom quickly added. "You have to pay me back."

Jessica was jumping around in circles. "Anything!"

"I want you to empty all the garbage cans at home," Mom said.

"No problem," Jessica said.

"And pull up the dandelions in the yard," Mom added.

Jessica was calming down a little. She hates to pull dandelions. "OK," she said.

"And vacuum the pool," Mom finished.

"Fine," Jessica said.

"Is it a deal?" Mom asked.

"Deal," Jessica said.

Mom and Jessica shook hands. Then Mom went to talk to the salesman.

"Do you think PizzaFace Three costs more than a Madame Zelda doll?" Jessica asked me.

"I don't know," I said.

"Well, I think it does," Jessica said.

"I'm not helping you do those chores," I told her.

"I don't care," Jessica said. "It's worth it. I can't wait until Lila opens our present. She's going to love it. Ellen will be so jealous!"

CHAPTER 8

Left-Out Lila

"Lila's party is tomorrow," Amy said before school on Friday.

"I know," I said. "It's going to be fun."

Amy, Todd, Eva, and I were watching Tinkerbell and Thumbelina. They are the class hamsters. Tinkerbell was running on the wheel. Thumbelina was drinking out of the water bottle. We had a new class pet, too. He was a bunny named Bugsy.

"What's your plan for the party?" Amy asked us.

"What do you mean?" Todd asked.

"Well, a lot is going to be happening

tomorrow," Amy said. "I don't want to waste time. So I'm planning out exactly what I want to do."

Todd thought about it for a minute. "I want plenty of time to eat," he said. "Lila said she's having chocolate cake. I'm going to have six pieces!"

Eva bent down to get a better look into the hamsters' cage. She didn't say anything. I hoped that didn't mean she had decided not to come to the party.

"I guess we'll have to watch Lila open her presents," Amy said. "I hope she's quick."

"Amy!" I said.

Amy's face turned red. "I'm sorry. I guess that was kind of mean."

I turned around and looked for Lila. I wanted to make sure she hadn't heard what Amy said.

Lila was sitting at her desk. Her head was down. She wasn't paying any attention to us.

Mrs. Otis arrived, and school started. I watched Lila all morning. She looked sad.

After lunch, I tried to play hopscotch with Ellen and Jessica.

"Who wants to go first?" I asked.

Jessica stepped forward. "I should."

"Why?" Ellen asked.

"Because I got the best present for Lila," Jessica said.

"Did not," Ellen said.

"*And* the best wrapping paper," Jessica added. "It's gold. And our ribbon is gold, too."

"Copycat!" Ellen yelled.

"I am not!" Jessica yelled.

"Are too," Ellen said. "I had silver paper before you had gold paper."

"Well, silver isn't the same as gold," Jessica argued.

"You got that paper just to make me mad," Ellen said.

"Why would I do that?" Jessica asked.

Ellen put her hands on her hips.

"Because you're jealous that my present is more expensive."

"No, I'm not!" Jessica yelled. "Because my present is more expensive."

I dropped my hopscotch stone. "I don't want to play anymore. I'll see you later."

Jessica and Ellen hardly noticed when I left.

I walked over to the swings. Lila was sitting on one. The rest were empty.

"Hi," I said.

"Hi," Lila said.

"You look sad," I said.

Lila shrugged.

"You should be excited," I said. "Your birthday is tomorrow."

Lila took a shaky breath. "No, it's not."

"What do you mean?" I asked.

Lila started to cry.

"What's wrong?" I asked.

"My birthday *party* is tomorrow." Lila licked a tear off her lip. "But my birthday is today."

"It is?" I asked. "Happy birthday!"

"Thanks." Lila was still crying. "You're the first person to tell me that. Even my dad forgot."

"Really?" I asked.

Lila nodded. "Dad was on the phone all during breakfast. He was talking to the baker who's making my cake."

"Didn't Jessica and Ellen say 'Happy birthday'?" I asked.

"No," Lila said. "They've hardly talked to me all day."

I looked over at the hopscotch board. Ellen and Jessica were still arguing.

Poor Lila. Everyone was so excited about her party, they had forgotten about her birthday. Of course, that was partly Lila's fault. She was the one who kept bragging about her party. Still, I felt sorry for her.

"Let's go tell Mrs. Otis it's your birthday," I suggested.

"No!" Lila wiped the tears off her

face. "I don't want you to tell anyone."

"Why not?" I asked.

"Just because," Lila said. "Promise?"

I sighed. "Promise." I was beginning to feel as if I knew too many secrets.

CHAPTER 9

Where's Eva?

"Wow!" Jessica exclaimed. "Look at the balloons."

"There must be hundreds," I said.

"I think *I* want to come to this party," Dad said.

Jessica and I laughed. We knew Dad was just kidding.

"I'll carry the present," Jessica announced. Mom had wrapped the video game in the gold paper and bow. It looked very pretty.

"OK," I agreed.

We climbed out of the car.

"Thanks, Dad," Jessica called.

"See you later," I called.

Dad beeped his horn and drove away.

A clown ran up to meet us. "Welcome to the party!" he said.

"Thank you," I said.

"Thanks," Jessica said.

"Come this way," the clown said with a big gesture. He skipped around the side of the house. Jessica and I followed him. I tried to skip just like the clown, but it was hard in my party dress.

"Look at the pool!" I exclaimed. Dozens of white candles were floating in it.

"It looks beautiful," Jessica cried.

"Have fun!" the clown said. He tooted his horn at us. Then he skipped back to the driveway to meet the next guest.

Two tents were set up in the Fowlers' backyard. One was bright red. The other had pink and white stripes.

A bunch of tables were under the red tent. One table was covered with presents. The others were piled high with food.

The ponies were under the pink-and-white tent. The people who were taking care of them were dressed up like cowboys.

Another clown was wandering around the yard. He was juggling bright-red balls.

"I can juggle better than that," Jessica said.

"Jessica!" I cried. "You hit Amy with your beanbag when you tried juggling!"

Jessica shrugged.

Most of the kids in our class had already arrived. I saw Todd near the food. Amy was riding a pony. But I didn't see Eva anywhere. My heart sank. I hoped she would be brave enough to come.

"What should we do first?" Jessica asked.

"Let's wish Lila a happy birthday," I said.

"Do you see her?" Jessica said.

I looked around. "There she is," I

told Jessica. "Near the presents."

Jessica and I walked over to Lila.

"Hi," I said. "Happy birthday."

Jessica put our present down on the table with the others. "Yeah, happy birthday," she said.

"Thanks." Lila wasn't smiling.

Amy ran up to us. "Hi, Elizabeth. Do you want to go on a pony ride? I've already been twice."

"I want to find Eva first," I said.

"She's not here yet," Amy said.

"Then I want to wait," I told her.

"OK." Amy sounded disappointed.

"I want a hot dog," Jessica announced.

Amy, Lila, and I each got a hot dog, too. Before we had finished eating them, Ellen arrived.

"Happy birthday, Lila," Ellen said. She held out her enormous silver present. It was much bigger than ours.

"Thanks," Lila said. "Just put your present on the table."

69

Ellen must have expected Lila to be more excited about the big box. She frowned as she put down the present.

"Come on," Amy said to me. "Let's ride the ponies. I don't think Eva is coming."

I hoped Amy was wrong. But I followed her to the pony tent. Jessica and Ellen wouldn't come. They wanted to stay near the presents.

"Aren't they cute?" Amy asked as I studied the ponies.

I nodded. "They're so small! They're much shorter than the horses at the stables."

"Would you like a ride?" one of the cowboys asked me.

"Yes, please," I said. "I'd like to ride the brown one with white feet."

"Fine," the cowboy said. He helped me into the pony's saddle. Then he led her around the ring.

"Are you having fun?" the cowboy asked me.

"Yup," I said.

"Are you scared?" he asked.

"No way," I said. "I take riding lessons."

"Should I let go?" the cowboy asked.

"Yes," I said.

The cowboy handed me the reins. I led the pony around the ring all by myself. Twice. I could see Mrs. Fowler filming me on a camera. I waved.

"Wasn't that fun?" Amy asked when I got off.

"Yes," I said.

But I wasn't really having a good time. I felt sorry for Lila. She still looked upset. And I was worried about Eva. Why hadn't she come? Had she decided her necklace wasn't good enough?

"Hey, there's Eva," Amy said.

I looked where Amy was pointing.

Eva was just arriving. She was carrying a small box. Hurray!

"I'll see you in a minute," I told Amy. I rushed across the lawn.

"Hi, Eva!" I yelled.

"Hi, Elizabeth!"

"I'm so glad you came," I told Eva. "Why are you so late?"

"I went to the doctor's with my dad," Eva explained.

"Really?" I said. "What did the doctor say?"

"He said Dad is much better," Eva told me. "He can go back to work soon."

"All right!" I said.

I felt happy. But I was a little nervous. I had talked Eva into coming. What if Lila laughed at her present? Eva would be angry with me.

I crossed my fingers and hoped everything turned out OK.

CHAPTER 10

Lots of Presents

"Come on, kids," one of the clowns told me and Eva. "It's time for the magician!"

"All right!" Eva said.

Eva and I sat next to each other on the grass. Jessica and Ellen sat behind us. They were still arguing about whose present was the best.

The magician pulled miles of scarves out of her hat. She made a deck of cards pop out of Andy Franklin's ear. She even cut Lila in half!

"She was terrific," Eva said when the show was over.

"Definitely," I agreed.

It was time for Lila to open her presents. Everyone walked to the Fowlers' living room. Some waiters had moved the presents inside

"Wow!" Eva's eyes widened when she saw the table loaded with gifts.

"Lila got a lot of presents," I said.

"They all look so fancy," Eva said. She glanced down at the little box she was still carrying.

"Don't worry," I said.

"OK," Eva whispered, sounding very worried. She put her present on the table with the others.

Ellen marched up to the table. "You should open the biggest presents first," she told Lila.

"Fine," Lila said. She didn't seem to care much.

Eva looked miserable. Her necklace was in the smallest box of all.

"Mine's biggest," Ellen announced.

"You have to open it first." She handed Lila the box.

Lila ripped open the fancy silver paper. She lifted out the doll.

"Do you like it?" Ellen asked eagerly.

"Sure," Lila said with a shrug. She put the doll down on the table.

"It's a Madame Zelda," Ellen said.

"I know," Lila said. She held out her hand for the next present.

Ellen looked really disappointed. I *almost* felt sorry for her.

Jessica stuck her tongue out at Ellen.

"She's going to like ours better," Jessica whispered to me.

Lila opened a few more presents. She didn't seem very happy with any of them.

Ellen handed Lila our gold box. "This one is next-biggest."

Lila unwrapped PizzaFace III. "Daddy already bought me this," she said.

Jessica's jaw dropped.

"I can't believe Lila didn't like those

fancy gifts!" Eva sounded really worried. "She's never going to like mine."

"Sure she will," I said. But I wasn't sure, either.

Lila unwrapped tons more presents—movie videos, posters, tapes, books, stuffed animals, clothes, and water toys.

A long time passed.

Eva's little box was the very last present.

Lila unwrapped the necklace. She smiled for the first time.

"This is so pretty!" Lila exclaimed. She looked for a card. But Eva hadn't put one on the box.

"Who's this from?" Lila asked.

Eva didn't answer. I turned toward her—but she was gone!

"Where's Eva?" I asked.

Jessica shrugged.

"Who gave me this?" Lila repeated.

"Eva did," I told her.

"Where is Eva?" Lila asked.

"I don't know," I said.

"Maybe she went to the bathroom," Ellen suggested.

"Or to ride the ponies," Amy said.

Lila pushed the wrapping paper and ribbons off her lap and stood up. "Let's find her!"

Everyone searched for Eva.

Jessica and I looked in the red tent.

Amy checked the pony tent.

Eva wasn't anywhere.

Todd wandered over to me. He was carrying a big bowl of chocolate ice cream. "What's going on?"

"We're looking for Eva," I explained. "She's missing."

"She left," Todd said.

Lila ran up to us. She was wearing the necklace Eva made. It *did* look pretty with her hair.

"Do you know where Eva is?" Lila asked Todd.

"She left," Todd repeated.

"Why would she do that?" Lila asked.

Todd shrugged. "I don't know. But she was crying."

"Crying?" Lila repeated. "I wonder why."

I sighed. "I think I know. But it's a long story. And I promised Eva I wouldn't tell."

Lila frowned. "Well, I'm going over to Eva's as soon as the party is over. I want to thank her for my necklace."

"Can I come, too?" I asked Lila.

"Sure," she said.

CHAPTER 11

The Best Present of All

"Happy birthday to you," everyone sang. "Happy birthday to you. Happy birthday, dear Lila. Happy birthday to you."

We all cheered.

Lila was standing behind an enormous cake. The candles were lighting up her face. She looked happy.

"Make a wish," Mr. Fowler said.

Lila closed her eyes and wished. Then she took a deep breath and blew out all of her candles.

We cheered again.

Everyone ate a piece of cake. Everyone

except for Todd. He ate *four* pieces.

"What about the other two?" Amy asked Todd. "You said you were going to eat six."

Todd put a hand on his belly and groaned. "I can't. I feel sick."

After that, the party was pretty much over. Some of the kids started to go home.

"Should we call Dad?" Jessica asked.

"Not yet," I said. "I want to go over to Eva's with Lila. We want to make sure she's OK."

"I'll come, too," Jessica said.

"Fine," I said.

Jessica and I stayed at Lila's until everyone else had left. Then Lila asked her father to drive us over to the Simpsons'. She told him it was important.

"No problem," Mr. Fowler said. "After all, it is the *day after* your birthday."

Lila giggled.

Mr. Fowler hadn't forgotten Lila's

birthday, after all! I was glad.

When we got to the Simpsons', Lila, Jessica, and I walked up to the door together. Mr. Fowler waited for us in the car.

Lila rang the bell.

A second later, Eva came to the door. She burst into tears when she saw us.

"I know why you're here," she told Lila. "I'm sorry! Please don't be mad at me."

"Why would I be mad?" Lila sounded surprised.

"Because of the present," Eva said. "I never should have given it to you. It wasn't good enough."

Lila shook her head. "The necklace is my favorite present of all. Look, I'm wearing it!"

"But I don't understand," Eva said. "You kept saying you wanted expensive presents. The necklace didn't cost a thing."

"I was wrong about the expensive presents," Lila said.

"Wait," Jessica said. "What do you mean it didn't cost anything?"

"Eva made it herself," I explained.

"Really?" Jessica was surprised. "That must have taken a long time."

"It did," I said. "Eva really worked hard."

"And Elizabeth helped," Eva said.

I couldn't help bragging a little. "It took us hours just to choose the shells. And then we had to string them. Eva really thought a lot about what Lila would like."

"Wow," Lila said softly. "You're the only one who thought so much about me."

"Well, you're the birthday girl," Eva pointed out. "It's your special day."

"Thank you," Lila said. "I'll wear it every day!"

Eva grinned. "You're welcome."

CHAPTER 12

Chores

"How could I be so stupid?" Jessica asked. "Why did I let Mom buy PizzaFace?"

"Let her?" I asked.

"OK," Jessica mumbled. "*Make* her."

It was a few days after Lila's party. Jessica was sitting in the grass pulling dandelions. She was finally starting the chores she had promised Mom she'd do.

"You thought Lila would like it," I said.

"Well, she didn't," Jessica answered. "And now I have to suffer."

I sat down next to Jessica. "Come on. It's not that bad. I'll help you."

"Thanks!" Jessica said. "Do you know what Lila told me today?"

"What?" I asked.

"She really wants a purple jacket," Jessica said. "Just like the one Mom wanted to buy. She said it would go with her new necklace!"

I lay back on the grass and laughed.

Jessica didn't join in.

That night, my family had dinner at Mr. Simpson's restaurant. It was the Grand Reopening.

Mr. Simpson was there. He was wearing an apron and cooking up a storm.

"Hi, Elizabeth!" Eva looked totally happy. "Hi, Jessica!"

"Hi," I said.

"I have something for you," Eva told me.

"You do?"

Eva nodded. She pulled a tiny box out from behind her back.

"Wow!" I carefully unwrapped the present. It was a shell bracelet, made just like Lila's necklace.

"It's a thank-you present," Eva told me.

"It's so pretty," I exclaimed.

"It sure is," Jessica said. "But remember—it's the thought that counts."

I stuck my tongue out at Jessica.

The Ritemans were eating at the restaurant that night, too. After dinner, the grown-ups ordered coffee. Ellen, Jessica, Eva, and I went out on the beach to play.

"What's the matter, Ellen?" I asked.

"You do seem gloomy," Eva added.

"Are you still mad about Lila's present?" Jessica asked.

Ellen shook her head. "No, that's not it. I just found out my cousin is coming to visit. For practically a whole week! She's even going to come to school with me."

"That sounds like fun," I said.

"Yeah," Jessica agreed.

"Well, it won't be fun," Ellen said. "I can't stand my cousin. And I'm sure you won't like her, either."

Jessica and I traded looks. Was Ellen's cousin really that bad?

Will Jessica and Elizabeth like Ellen's cousin? Find out in Sweet Valley Kids #59, *Jessica+Jessica= Trouble*.

SIGN UP FOR THE
SWEET VALLEY HIGH®
FAN CLUB!

Hey, girls! Get all the gossip on Sweet
Valley High's® most popular teenagers
when you join our fantastic Fan Club!
As a member, you'll get all of this really
cool stuff:

- Membership Card with your own
  personal Fan Club ID number
- A Sweet Valley High® Secret
  Treasure Box
- Sweet Valley High® Stationery
- Official Fan Club Pencil (for secret
  note writing!)
- Three Bookmarks
- A "Members Only" Door Hanger
- Two Skeins of J. & P. Coats® Embroidery
  Floss with flower barrette instruction
  leaflet
- Two editions of *The Oracle* newsletter
- Plus exclusive Sweet Valley High®
  product offers, special savings,
  contests, and much more!

Be the first to find out what Jessica & Elizabeth Wakefield are up to by joining the
Sweet Valley High® Fan Club for the one-year membership fee of only $6.25 each
for U.S. residents, $8.25 for Canadian residents (U.S. currency). Includes shipping
& handling.

Send a check or money order (do not send cash) made payable to "Sweet Valley
High® Fan Club" along with this form to:

SWEET VALLEY HIGH® FAN CLUB, BOX 3919-B, SCHAUMBURG, IL 60168-3919

NAME _____
           (Please print clearly)

ADDRESS _____

CITY_____ STATE _____ ZIP_____
                                                        (Required)

AGE _____ BIRTHDAY_____ / _____ / _____